The
Sleeping Giant

Marie-Louise Fitzpatrick

THE O'BRIEN PRESS

DUBLIN

Long ago, when Ireland was still on the edge of the world, there was a giant living in the Kingdom of Kerry. He was large as giants go, but a friendly, happy sort of fellow.

Unfortunately, he was also rather noisy and he got in the way quite a bit.

It wasn't his fault, of course, and all the people liked him, but he was *so* awkward!

When he went for a walk the earth shook for miles around. His big feet were
forever knocking down farm walls and trees. And when he lay down to sleep,
well, he really did pick his places!

The people of Kerry went to the King.

'Something must be done about the big fellow!' they yelled.

The King paid a visit to the druid.

'Something must be done about the big fellow!' said the King, handing the druid a bag of gold.

The druid said he would see what he could do.

He made a big cauldron of stew and put in special herbs to make the giant sleep. Then he invited the giant to dinner.

The meal was delicious and the giant ate three huge helpings.

Soon the giant was feeling drowsy.

'Go out into the sea and lie down out of the way, big fellow,' said the druid.

The giant waded out into the waves and lay down.

'Lovely meal, Druid. A bit heavy on the herbs, mind. You must dine with me sometime soon,' he mumbled as he drifted off to sleep.

The secret potion was very strong. Years went by and the giant slept on.

Brendan the Navigator set off on his travels, the great Spanish Armada floundered on the west coast, but still the giant slept.

Grass grew over him, animals made their homes on him, seabirds nested on his sides.

People forgot that he was really a giant and thought he was an island. Some called the island 'The Sleeping Giant' and others called it 'The Dead Man'. The island became quite famous and people came from far and wide to see it.

Then, one day, the sleeping giant woke up!

He opened his eyes and yawned. He stood up and stretched.

He'd had a nice long sleep and now he felt like a nice long chat!

He looked around him. There were lots of people on Coumeenole Beach so he waded ashore to say hello.

Well! When the people on the beach saw the big fellow coming towards them, there was uproar!

There was screaming and shouting and people running everywhere. And then – the beach was empty.

Except for the poor old giant.

'How strange,' he thought. 'You'd think they'd never seen a giant before!'

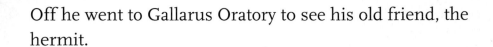

Off he went to Gallarus Oratory to see his old friend, the hermit.

But the hermit was long gone and now the place was full of tourists.

The giant leaned down to say hello – but all the tourists ran away!

Then he heard music coming from a nearby pub and he went to listen.

There was a great session in full swing. Musicians were playing, everyone was singing – the whole pub was laughing and talking.

Now, the big fellow loved music but he couldn't hear it properly, so...

...he lifted the roof off.

Pandemonium!

When the people looked up and saw a giant, why, the house was cleared in seconds!

Oh, the poor big fellow!

He did so want to sit and chat with someone after being asleep for so long. But no one would talk to him.

Why, they wouldn't even stay around long enough to say hello.

The giant felt very lonely and upset.

He wandered off to a deserted valley where no one had lived since the Great Famine.

He sat down by himself and cried and cried.

He cried so much that big clouds formed around his head. It began to rain.

And rain.

Oh, how it rained!

It rained all over Kerry and everyone got very wet.

The fishermen grumbled that the seas were too rough.

The locals complained that they couldn't go out for fear of bumping into the giant.

The tourists complained that there was no famous island to photograph anymore.

And last thing at night, when the National Anthem was played on television, the sun had no island to sink behind.

It just went straight into the sea!

The people went to the Tourist Board and said that something must be done about the giant. The man from the Tourist Board agreed.

'We can't have a giant running around ruining the tourist trade,' he said. 'He'll have to be made go back to sleep in the sea.'

'Yes, yes,' shouted the crowd.

'Someone will have to tell him to go away,' said the man.

'Yes, yes,' shouted the crowd.

'Any volunteers?' asked the man.

'Not likely!' muttered the crowd.

Then a little girl called Ann piped up. 'I'll talk to the giant,' she said.

So the little girl was flown in a helicopter to the valley.

She was lowered down and there was the poor giant, still crying his eyes out.

'It would be so much fun to have a wide awake giant for a friend,' thought Ann sadly. But she knew the people would never put up with him. She had to get him safely back into the sea.

'Hello, big fellow,' she said. 'Why are you crying?'

'No one likes me,' sobbed the giant.

'Yes, they do,' said Ann. 'When you were an island people came from all over the world to take pictures of you asleep in the sea.'

'Really?' sniffed the giant.

'Yes, and the fishermen were always talking about you and we read legends about you in school. You're on television every night too.'

'Really?' said the giant, stopping his tears.

'Yes,' said Ann. 'Everyone is very sad now because you are not in the sea anymore.'

'Is that so?' said the giant, beginning to cheer up. 'Well, then I must go back and lie down again.'

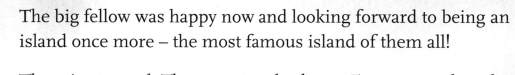

The big fellow was happy now and looking forward to being an island once more – the most famous island of them all!

The rain stopped. The sun came back out. Everyone gathered on the cliffs to say goodnight to the giant.

They held a big party for him and made his favourite vegetable stew. The musicians from the pub were there; they played for hours and hours.

Ann was there too, of course.

Ah, that was a night to remember.

At last the giant felt very tired and he lay down to sleep in the sea for another while.

'Goodnight, everyone,' said the giant.

'Goodnight, big fellow!' yelled the people.

'Great party,' said the giant, yawning. 'The stew was nearly as good as the druid's, but there was something missing. Not enough herbs...'

He closed his eyes.

'Goodnight, little Ann,' he mumbled as he drifted off to sleep.

'Goodnight, big fellow,' said Ann. 'Sleep well.'